MR. BUMP
and the Knight

KT-217-215

Roger Hargreaves

Original concept by
Roger Hargreaves

Written and illustrated by
Adam Hargreaves

Mr Bump was thoroughly fed up. It did not seem to matter what he did, he always ended up getting bumped and bruised or scraped and scratched.

So, you can imagine how hard it was for him to find a job.

He had tried working at the baker's, but he had burnt his fingers on the bread oven.

OUCH!

He had tried being a bricklayer, but he had dropped a brick on his foot.

THUD!

OUCH!

He had even tried working at the pillow factory.

Who could hurt themselves in a pillow factory?

Mr Bump, of course!

He got a feather in his eye!

OUCH!

Every day it was bandage this and bandage that.
Poor Mr Bump was very fed up.

Then one day, while Mr Bump was walking in the woods behind his house, he met someone who gave him a wonderful idea.

The perfect idea for a new job.

That someone was a Knight in shining armour, riding by on his horse.

Now, it was not the thought of the excitement and adventure of being a Knight that caught Mr Bump's imagination, nor was it the idea of the fame and fortune he might win. No, it was the Knight's solid, metal armour that caught his eye.

Shining armour that protected the Knight from bumps and bruises, scrapes and scratches.

"If I wore armour like that," thought Mr Bump to himself, "I would never need to worry about bumping myself again. I shall become a Knight."

Early the next morning, Mr Bump rushed to the blacksmith's to buy himself a suit of armour.

The blacksmith had to put the armour on very carefully to avoid Mr Bump's bruises, but when he had it on, Mr Bump looked at his reflection in the mirror and smiled.

Mr Bump then bought a book called 'Knights, All You Need to Know'.

"Now," said Mr Bump, opening the book, "what do Knights do?"

He read a whole chapter about jousting. Then he went out and bought a horse and a lance and went to a local jousting tournament.

However, Mr Bump quickly found out that he was not very good at jousting. Every time he sat on his horse he fell off.

CRASH!

The other Knights thought it was hilarious.

That evening, Mr Bump opened his book and read a chapter called 'Saving Damsels in Distress'.

The next day, he set off, on foot, to find a damsel in need of saving.

Fortunately, because it was very awkward walking in a suit of armour, Mr Bump found one near his house.

A damsel locked in a very tall tower.

"Will you save me, Sir Knight?" cried the Damsel.

"I will!" Mr Bump called back.

The Damsel let down a ladder woven from her long, fine hair.

But try as hard as he might, Mr Bump could not climb the ladder.

He kept falling off at every attempt.

BANG! CRASH! CLUNK!

Feeling rather sorry for himself, and even more sorry for the Damsel, Mr Bump trudged off home.

The next chapter in the book was entitled 'Slaying Dragons'.

"That's the one for me!" cried Mr Bump.

The following day, Mr Bump bought a sword and shield and went in search of a dragon. There were not any near by, so he caught the bus.

The dragon was asleep on the top of a steep hill.

It took Mr Bump a lot of huffing and puffing to climb to the top.

When he finally reached the top, he raised his sword above his head to slay the dragon, but the weight of the sword tipped Mr Bump off balance.

With a great CRASHING and CLATTERING of armour, he rolled all the way down the hill.

It was a very sad Mr Bump who got back home later that day.

He had to face the fact that he was not cut out to be a Knight.

He went up to his bedroom and took off his armour.

And then he noticed something quite remarkable.

When he glimpsed himself in the mirror, it was a very different Mr Bump looking back at him

A Mr Bump without a bandage or a plaster in sight.

A Mr Bump without a bump or a bruise.

Mr Bump smiled.

And then he laughed . . .

. . . and then he fell over backwards and bumped his head on the bed!